Greta Gorsuch
NEWCOMERS

Greta Gorsuch has taught ESL/EFL and Applied Linguistics for more than thirty-five years in Japan, Vietnam, and the United States. Greta's work has appeared in journals such as *System*, *Language Teaching Research*, and *TESL-EJ*. She is currently co-editor of *Reading in a Foreign Language*. Her books in the Gemma Open Door series include *The Cell Phone Lot*, *Key City on the River*, *Post Office on the Tokaido*, and *The Night Telephone*. She is co-author of *Using Theories for Second Language Teaching and Learning* (Bloomsbury). Greta lives in beautiful, wide West Texas and she goes camping whenever she can.

First published by Gemma in 2023.

www.gemmamedia.org

©2023 by Greta Gorsuch

All rights reserved. No part of this publication may be reproduced in any manner whatsoever without written permission from the publisher, except in the case of brief quotations embodied in critical articles or reviews.

Printed in the United States of America

978-1-956476-24-8

Library of Congress Cataloging-in-Publication Data is available.

Cover by Laura Shaw Design

Named after the brightest star in the Northern Crown, Gemma is a nonprofit organization that helps new readers acquire English language literacy skills with relevant, engaging books, eBooks, and audiobooks. Always original, never adapted, these stories introduce adults and young adults to the life-changing power of reading.

GEMMA

Open Door

Chapter 1

Ababio Ollennu sat in airport shuttle bus number 36. Its engine rumbled. It was not the good rumble of a new engine. In fact, the rumble was loud. The windows of the shuttle bus rattled and shook. Blue smoke came out the back of the bus. Ababio thought the engine could stop any time it liked. And then, not start up again. He hoped he was not driving when *that* happened. He could call the airport shuttle office. He could ask for help, of course. But the Dallas/Fort Worth International Airport was huge. It had hundreds of miles of roads. The airport also had hundreds of shuttle buses. It might take hours for help to come.

The last time Ababio looked, shuttle bus number 36 had over three hundred thousand miles on it. It was old and tired. It had hard seats. Its carpet had no color anymore. Number 36 smelled like old fried food. Still, it was better than any truck he drove in Ghana. In his college days in Kumasi he sometimes took trucking jobs with his cousin Folami. He needed the money. They moved old clothes, fresh fruit, and sometimes goats or chickens. Those trucks were so old you could not see how many miles were on them. He saw one truck stuck at three hundred fifty thousand miles. He was sure it had many more miles than that.

Once, after taking twenty-four goats to another city, the owner of the truck shouted at Ababio and Folami. "Wash out this truck!" he shouted. "The goats have pooped all over it!"

"Not our fault, man," Folami answered in his lazy voice. "Goats get terribly excited in a truck. They poop."

But the truck's owner kept shouting. Finally, Ababio and Folami got buckets of water. They washed out the goat poop from the back of the truck. Ababio did most of the work. It was always that way with his cousin Folami.

But now Ababio was in America. He had finished a master's degree at an American university. It was in West Texas, three hundred miles from Dallas. No one in Ghana had ever heard of it. It was not a famous school. But after two hard years, Ababio was done. Now he was looking for a job as a high school science teacher. He wanted to work in the "big city," Dallas. He graduated in August. It was too late to get a September job at a school. But two schools told him they would talk to him in November. He could start in January. That was two months away.

For now, driving a shuttle bus at the Dallas/Fort Worth International Airport was okay. The money was okay. And sometimes the work was interesting. His driving assignment this morning was at the airport employee parking lot. The job was simple. He waited at the parking lot. Then workers got out of their cars. Some got off a city bus from Dallas or Fort Worth. Then they walked to Ababio's shuttle bus. They sat and talked for a few minutes. Ababio had to wait until he had fifteen workers. When he had fifteen, he took them to the airport employee security checkpoint. Then they went through security. After that they walked away to one of their many jobs in the huge airport. The airport really was like a city.

Ababio waited. Workers got onto shuttle bus number 36 and sat down. They had to talk loudly over the rumbling, rattling engine. Many talked in English, the one language they shared. But Ababio also heard two or three other languages he did not know. He laughed. Here they were, in the second largest airport in America. And every single worker on his bus spoke another language as their mother tongue.

Chapter 2

On his second trip to the employee parking lot, Ababio saw some people he knew. They were waiting for the shuttle bus. The shuttle bus stop had a kind of umbrella over it. Today, everyone stood under it. It was only 8:00 a.m. But the early September sun was already hot. This was Ababio's third summer in Texas. Summers were hot and bright. The heat stayed. It was like Ghana. He didn't mind. But for his airport friends from China, it was different. It was just too hot for them. One of them, Wei Zhang, turned pink in the heat. Outside, he had to wipe his face with a towel all the time. Inside, with air-conditioning, he was better.

Wei Zhang worked at a massage spa in the airport. He was a young guy. He spoke little English. Last week he showed Ababio a white card. The white card had all the English he knew. The card said, "Soft or hard?" and "Is that sore?" and "Everything okay?" and "Okay done now." Wei Zhang got the card from his massage school in California. "Soft or hard?" meant "Do you want a soft massage?" or "Do you want a hard massage?" "Is that sore?" was supposed to be used if a customer said "Ow!" or "That hurt!" And in the massage spa business, it was important to ask customers, "Is everything okay?"

Ababio took the card and added a few sentences for Wei Zhang to try. One was "How's it going?" Another was "Wow it's really hot today, isn't it?" Ababio's favorite was "See you next time." When Wei Zhang got on shuttle bus number 36 this morning, he said to Ababio, "How's it going?"

"It's going good man!" Ababio said. He gave Wei Zhang a big grin. Wei Zhang wiped his face with his white towel and sat down.

A second person got on the shuttle bus. It was a young woman. Ababio thought she was from Bangladesh or India. He wasn't sure. She wore a long dress. It covered her arms all the way to her hands. Her hair was completely covered with a dark cloth. She wore glasses. She told Ababio she worked at Moon Lake Coffee. Moon Lake Coffee had shops all over the airport. Everyone went to Moon Lake Coffee. They waited in long lines to order their drinks. Then they walked fast to this gate or that gate. Everyone was on their way somewhere.

It took a little time for Ababio to understand the young woman's English. She talked very softly and very fast. "Moon Lake Coffee" sounded like "moonlakecoffee." She never gave her name. This morning, Ababio said, "Hello." The young woman didn't answer. She walked past Wei Zhang and sat down on one of the hard seats. She looked out the window. Outside it was just a hot parking lot with cars. Beyond were dozens of jet planes waiting to take off. One jet plane flew right overhead. For a minute, you couldn't hear anything but the roar of the jet engines. The shuttle windows rattled hard. The young woman's face changed not at all.

Two more young women got on. Ababio knew one of them. She was Min Li. She was from China. Like Wei Zhang, she had a hard time with the hot sun. Sometimes she had her own umbrella. Or she wore a pretty hat. But unlike Wei Zhang, Min Li knew a lot of English. "Oh! I thought I was late!" she said. She wore her usual cute clothes. She had style. She had to dress up for her job. She sold expensive clothes at a shop in the airport. "I want to be a fashion designer!" she once told Ababio. He wasn't surprised.

Ababio didn't know the other young woman. She was short. She had long black hair that was pulled back. She smiled. Ababio smiled back. She walked to where Min Li was and they both sat down. Who was this new person? Ababio looked back into shuttle bus number 36. He had fifteen people. It was time to go. He pulled away, and a cloud of blue smoke followed.

Chapter 3

Rosa Maria Garza sat next to her friend, Min Li. It was her first day at the Dallas/Fort Worth International Airport. She had a new job at a bookstore at the airport. Min Li was her friend at West River Community College. They were in English class together. Both of them could speak English, but their writing and reading needed work. Rosa needed to write and read English better so she could begin nursing school next year. Her dream was to be a nurse. She wanted to wear a nurse's uniform. She loved medicine. She wanted to help people. The newspaper in her hometown of Puebla, Mexico, had many reports that hospitals in the US and Canada needed nurses.

Her father grew avocadoes and cotton in the mountains outside of Puebla. Her mother was a teacher. They had a little money to help Rosa. "We can help you," her father said. "But we ask a few things."

"Okay," she answered.

"First," he said, "you have to live in Dallas with my brother Roberto."

"Oh," Rosa said. Her uncle Roberto owned a car repair shop in Dallas. He had two kids under the age of ten. And he had a new wife. She was going to have a baby soon.

"I know what you're thinking," her father said. "Small kids, small house,

Roberto talks too much, and all that. But we've decided. You can save money by living with them. Roberto says you will have your own room."

"Okay," she said. She knew her father was not finished.

"One more thing," her father said. "You have to find a job when you get there. The only way we can do this is if you also make money."

"Oh," Rosa said. That wasn't so bad. She had been working since she was fourteen. Rosa loved medicine. But even more, Rosa loved books. It was no surprise her first job was at a bookstore. She was lucky. Her mother's friend at school had a bookstore, and she took on Rosa. Rosa carried books to customers. She answered their questions. She helped the owner put out new books for customers to look at.

Rosa's mother then spoke. "Are you sure you want to go to El Norte? Is that really what you want? It's a bad place for anyone from Mexico." "El Norte" meant "The North." This was what they called the United States.

"It's a bad place for anyone from Guatemala or El Salvador," Rosa's father said.

Rosa answered, "Yes, true. But Uncle Roberto lives in Dallas. He does all right."

Rosa's parents looked at each other. "Yes . . ." her father finally said.

Uncle Roberto's house was small. His two kids, Maria and Bernardo, were young and noisy. Uncle Roberto talked a lot. His car repair business was doing well. Roberto's new wife was pretty and kind. But she was also tired with a baby coming. She needed help around the house.

Being in El Norte was harder than Rosa thought. But the one bright spot was her English classes at West River Community College. She made a good friend, Min Li. Min Li was quick to tell her about part-time jobs at the Dallas/Fort Worth International Airport.

"You can apply for a job online!" Min Li said. "Look here." She pulled out her pink cell phone and pushed a few buttons. Six airport job websites popped up. It took Rosa five minutes to find a job at a bookstore in the airport. It took her ten minutes to apply. In thirty minutes, the bookstore manager texted her. She wanted to meet Rosa. In twenty-four hours, Rosa sat with Min Li on a big old shuttle bus. She was on her way to her new job.

Chapter 4

Rosa went through the airport employee security checkpoint with no trouble. The security guards looked at her passport. Then they looked at her school card. She showed them her phone. They looked at the texts from the bookstore manager. One female security guard looked through her purse and her book bag.

"Studying English?" she asked, holding up Rosa's textbook.

"Yes," Rosa said. "I'm trying to, anyway."

"Great!" the female guard said. "Are you at West River Community College? I saw the school library sticker on your book."

"Yes!" Rosa said.

The female guard said, "Me too. Working on my degree for police work." The lady was in her late twenties with short brown hair.

"Maybe I'll see you there," Rosa said.

"Uh-huh. Have a great day." The guard waved Rosa Maria forward.

Rosa waited for Min Li. On the shuttle bus, Min Li told her, "The airport is huge. It's so busy! I got lost all the time at first. But don't worry. I'll show you where to go! Just wait for me after the security check!" With her dark shiny hair and perfect skin, Min Li looked fashionable and beautiful. But her beauty was more than that. Part of it was that she looked and sounded so happy. Nothing ever seemed to bother Min Li.

The security checkpoint opened up

to a large hall. Rosa looked to the right and could not see the end. The hall went on and on. It curved away into the far distance. She looked to the left, and it was the same. Rosa had never seen anything like it. Sure, her hometown of Puebla had a large town square. It was the center of Puebla's life. There was the church, the government buildings, the fountains, the businesses, and the cafes and candy shops. The Puebla town square was huge. But it wasn't endless like this hallway.

The hall was filled with people. There were hundreds and hundreds of them. It was like festival day in Puebla. Hundreds of Poblanos (people of Puebla) would be out. They would be walking slowly around the town square. But at the Dallas/Fort Worth International Airport, everyone was moving fast. Everyone was going somewhere. Some were talking on cell phones. Some people pulled small bags on rollers behind them. A few people were running. Rosa saw flight crews, men and women wearing airline uniforms. She saw people who were traveling for business. A few of the men and women wore suits. She saw many other people wearing blue jeans. One lady wore workout clothes like she was going to the gym. A few men wore cowboy hats and boots. One girl wore gold shorts and a tiny top that covered very little.

Rosa saw family groups. She saw a group of very old ladies walking slowly.

She heard a man shout, "Look out

for the cart! Look out for the cart!" A large cart came by. It was filled with more old people. The driver was a man from India or Egypt. Rosa could not tell which. As he passed, he called again, "Look out for the cart!"

Another airport employee, a man, passed by. He was pushing a wheelchair with an old man in it.

"OK, I'm through!" Min Li said. As if from nowhere, she was standing next to Rosa. "Are you ready for your first day at the airport?"

"Oh my God," Rosa said.

"I know," Min Li said. "It's a lot of people, isn't it? Just all kinds of people."

Chapter 5

Kaleda Zia was in line at the airport employee security checkpoint. It seemed to take longer every day. She carried a purse and a book bag. She wore her long dress, and her shirt and jacket. She wore her hijab. She tied it carefully over her head and around her neck. Just her face showed. She carefully tucked each piece of her black hair under the hijab. Only her hands showed. She was dressed perfectly and correctly. So then why did it always take so long at the security checkpoint?

Kaleda saw the Chinese girl and her friend ahead in line today. They had purses and book bags, too. The security guard looked through them quickly. The female guard asked a few questions, the young women answered, and then both were done. Just like that! But when it was *Kaleda's* turn, the lady guard seemed so slow. She asked Kaleda questions. Today she asked, "Where are you from?" and "How long have you been working here?" Kaleda answered each question with a single word. Or the shortest possible sentence. She said, "Bangladesh," and "Six weeks." The guard kept saying "What? What?" Kaleda repeated her answers in exactly the same way, soft and quick. It didn't seem to help. She couldn't understand why the guard asked her such questions. There was nothing wrong with her answers. Her English was good! She had top marks in her girls' school in Rangpur. When she went to college in Dhaka, the big capital city, she studied science *in English*. She had top marks there, too. She had gotten into a master's program at an American university.

Finally, the female security guard said, "All right. We're done here." Kaleda left the security checkpoint. She kept her head down. She turned right into the big hall and started walking to her job. She bumped into a few people. Each time she moved away without saying anything. She didn't look at the other person. Then she started walking again. This was what she did in her college days in Dhaka. It was a crowded city. You were a girl from a small town. You kept your eyes down. You kept walking. To Kaleda, walking in the Dallas/Fort Worth International Airport was no different. Ahead of Kaleda, a lady stopped to look at something in her hand. And Kaleda bumped right into her.

"Ooof!" the woman said. Then, "Excuse me! Are you all right?" She was an American, in her early thirties. Kaleda looked at the lady in the dark slacks and green blouse. She had an airport employee name tag. But Kaleda looked just for a second. Did she know the lady? It was best to keep walking. She was due in Moon Lake Coffee shop number seven in just a few minutes. She moved off without saying anything.

Kaleda made it to Moon Lake Coffee shop number seven without bumping into any more people. It was her first time at this store. She worked at shop number six last week. It was shop number two the week before that. There were nine Moon Lake Coffee shops in the Dallas/Fort Worth International Airport. She saw a long line of people at the front door of number seven. It was morning. A lot of people wanted something to drink. She smelled coffee. She pulled her hijab over her nose. Coffee was not a smell she liked. Good girls from good families in Bangladesh did not drink coffee alone in shops. They drank tea at home. In coffee shops, anyone could look at you. It wasn't the right thing for a girl. But here in America, Moon Lake Coffee was the only job she could get. She had to make money. She had left the master's degree program just a few months ago. Well, actually the MA program had dropped her. She could not keep her grades up. She had to hide that from her family in Bangladesh. They must never know! "Kaleda, Kaleda, what have you done?" she could hear her mother say. "And you were top girl in Rangpur School!"

Thinking of this, Kaleda went to the back of the Blue Moon Coffee shop. She stood so the two workers in the shop could see her. One of them would tell her what to do. She waited. But neither of the two women looked over at her. They were busy with customers. They moved fast, but the line of customers stayed long.

Someone tapped Kaleda on the arm. She jumped.

"Hello," the lady said. It was the same American lady Kaleda had bumped into, in the airport hall.

Chapter 6

Wei Zhang got through the security check quickly. He understood almost nothing of what the officers asked. However, he was at work six and seven days a week. The security officers got used to seeing him. He arrived early in the morning. At night, he didn't leave until 6:00 or 7:00 p.m. So, one set of morning security officers knew him. A second set of evening security officers also knew him. Both sets of officers saw a young, good-looking Chinese guy. Every day he wore black pants and a blue AirSpa shirt.

When he first started working for AirSpa, Wei Zhang made a decision. No matter what someone said to him, he would say "Uh-huh" and nod his head. He would also smile. That seemed to work pretty well. His communication style helped with two things. First, it saved him from having to say very much. This was good. His English was horrible. And second, just nodding and saying "Uh-huh" made people think he was listening. He worked as a massage therapist. Usually there was no need to talk. But sometimes a customer did want to talk. Wei Zhang would say "Uh-huh" and the customer would keep talking. It seemed to make them happy. Wei Zhang could hear lots of English without having to give answers. In the weeks and months he worked, he listened. He started to hear words and sentences. He could guess when a customer was talking about his flight. He now knew the words "flight" and "delay." When one female customer said, "Oh my feet are killing me!" he heard "my feet." He guessed that her feet hurt. When he massaged the customer's feet gently, she gave him a ten dollar cash tip.

Cash tips were everything. The AirSpa company paid almost nothing. The owner, a Chinese man with bad teeth, visited Wuhan, Wei Zhang's town. He was looking for young Chinese workers who wanted a new start in the US. Wuhan was perfect for the AirSpa owner to visit. It was a big city with a lot of young people and a lot of low-paying jobs. Like many young Chinese people, Wei Zhang didn't want to work in a car factory. He didn't want to make smartphones with a thousand other workers in white uniforms.

The AirSpa owner rented a room at the Wuhan City Hall and put out some notices: "Great jobs in the USA! Be a massage therapist in Dallas! Visas, air tickets, all included! Come to the information meeting!" Wei Zhang's friend told him about the AirSpa notice. Wei Zhang went to the meeting. There were ten other young Chinese men and women waiting there. The owner told Wei Zhang he would give him an air ticket, massage training in California, and a place to live in Dallas. He would handle the visa to work in the US. But in return, Wei Zhang had to work for him for ten months. This was to pay off the expenses of the air ticket, the training, the apartment, and the visa.

When Wei Zhang finally arrived in Dallas four months later, the AirSpa owner showed him an old, dirty apartment near the airport. There were twelve male massage therapists living there. They all had to share one bathroom and two bedrooms. Their beds were mattresses and blankets on the floor. The AirSpa owner lit a cigarette. He said, "Here's your bus card. Here's directions to work. Here's your schedule. Seven days a week, ten hours each day. If you do well, we can put you to six days a week."

Wei Zhang said, "When do I get paid?"

The owner puffed on his cigarette and said in a lazy voice, "Soon, soon. There's food in the kitchen. See? A big bag of rice, too. Good luck!" Then he left. For the next month, the only money Wei Zhang got was from cash tips customers gave him.

This morning, Wei Zhang walked through the crowded hall of the airport terminal. Any street in China was like this. Thousands of people walking fast, talking on their phones, and going somewhere. He was used to that. But he enjoyed how bright and clean the airport halls were. He liked the clear blue sky outside the big windows.

He got to the AirSpa shop. It was only 9:00 a.m., but one customer, a large American man in a business suit, was already waiting. A few others were already sitting in the special massage chairs getting a massage. One of the massage workers waved and smiled, and then got back to work.

Chapter 7

It took only a few minutes for Rosa to find the bookstore. The clothing store where Min Li worked was just one minute away. Min Li said, "Just keep walking that way! The bookstore's on the right. Maybe you can help them with their front window. It's pretty boring!" She laughed. With her pretty black hair swinging, she turned and walked into the clothing store.

Min Li was right. The front window of V.S. Carter Booksellers *was* boring. People went past without looking at the bookstore. It had a large front entrance. The front window was in the center of the entrance. It was supposed to make the shop look like an old-fashioned bookstore in New York or London. Like a place where you could sit down, rest, and read. Rosa suddenly felt homesick. She thought about the bookstore in Puebla. She missed the big bright front window filled with books. She missed the bookstore cat, a large gray thing that slept a lot.

The V.S. Carter Booksellers front window was small, and the dusty glass and the low lighting made it even smaller. You could hardly see it in the bright and busy airport hall. As Rosa watched, a lady airline pilot bumped into it. She was walking fast. When she checked her watch, her shoulder bumped into the edge of the dark front window. The dusty glass rattled. She dropped her coffee. "Ay no!" Rosa thought. The lady pilot never missed a step. She bent over, picked up her coffee cup, put it into the trash, and kept walking.

Rosa went past the dusty front window and into the bookstore. There was only one customer. An older man was looking at the politics books. They were on a big table. Some had pictures of different presidents on them. Others had pictures of the White House, or the Capitol building in Washington, D.C. Rosa saw one book with a picture of "the wall" between the US and Mexico.

Rosa looked for the owner. Finally, far in the back of the store, she found Elizabeth Carter. She was a short lady with a gray suit and glasses.

"Hi Ms. Carter," Rosa said. "I'm pleased to meet you."

"Ms. Garza! It's good you're here," Elizabeth Carter said. "Did you have a hard time getting here?"

"No, it was fine," Rosa said. "A friend from college helped me. She works just down the hall."

"Very good! You can put your bags back here," Elizabeth Carter said. She opened a small door and showed Rosa where to put her purse and book bag. The small room had boxes of books and a small desk. Rosa could see two large chairs all the way in the back. They were covered in books. Elizabeth Carter looked at Rosa. She took in Rosa's young, clean face. Rosa's dark hair was pulled back. She wore small silver hoop earrings. She was wearing dark slacks and a light green summer sweater. Her hands were small, and her nails were short, clean, and pink.

"I see you have a book bag with you," Elizabeth Carter said. "What are you reading?"

"Oh!" Rosa said. "One is to get ready for nursing school. The other one is *La Historia de Mis Dientes* by Valeria Luiselli. She's an author from Mexico City. But I'm reading it in English."

"*Dientes*? Is that something about teeth?" Elizabeth Carter asked.

"Ah yes," Rosa laughed. "It's *The Story of My Teeth* in English."

"Hmmm . . . and there's an English translation? That's something to think about for the store. One of the gates just over there has flights to Mexico City and La Paz twice a day. Maybe some customers will want to read new fiction from Mexican writers," Elizabeth Carter said. "All right then! Let's get you started. Here is the credit card machine. Have you used one before?"

Chapter 8

Shuttle bus number 36 shook and rattled. The engine really did sound worse. "Thrumm . . . POP! Thrumm . . . . Thrr . . . . . . THRUMMM," went the engine. It was so loud the employees couldn't talk to each other. They had to shout. Ababio Ollennu finished his thirty-first trip from the employee parking lot to the airport employee security checkpoint. He dropped off fifteen employees.

One of them, Mr. Hasim from Egypt, shouted, "That engine sounds bad!"

"Yes it does!" Ababio shouted back. Mr. Hasim waved goodbye and went into the security checkpoint.

Ababio was getting hungry. It was now 1:30 p.m. He called the airport shuttle service office and told them he was stopping for lunch. He pulled into the airport shuttle parking lot. He turned off the engine. He shut his eyes and waited to see what would happen. For a few seconds the engine kept making its sound. "THRUM . . . . . . thrum . . . . thr . . ." Then the shuttle engine stopped. Ababio waited a few more seconds. CLUNK! The shuttle bus jerked forward. A book an employee left on a seat fell to the floor.

Ababio waited a few more seconds. Nothing. He took a breath. Yes, shuttle bus number 36 was off. He wished he could repair the shuttle bus engine. With an MS in physics he ought to be able to repair an engine! In Ghana, he kept all sorts of impossible old trucks running. He thought he could give this shuttle bus engine a little more life. But his boss, Mr. Vernon Hackberry, said no. Mr. Hackberry wanted his son, Vern Junior, to repair the shuttle bus engine. Vern Junior was learning to be a truck mechanic at the West River Community College. As part of his mechanics course, he could repair the engine for free. His father, Mr. Vernon Hackberry, liked that idea very much.

Ababio walked back onto the shuttle bus. His job was to pick up trash, or anything else someone forgot. He picked up the book that fell on the floor. It was called *The Story of My Teeth*. Ababio looked for a name inside the book. But there was no name. He saw "West River Community College Library" printed on the side of the book. He knew his friend, Min Lee, went to English classes at West River. Maybe the book was hers.

Ababio finished cleaning up inside the old shuttle bus. He walked into the airport shuttle service office. Mr. Vernon Hackberry sat behind his desk. He didn't look up as Ababio came in. Vern Junior was there, too. He was texting on his cell phone. He was a large boy, about nineteen. His brown hair was cut very short. His face and neck were red from the hot Dallas sun. The black "Airport Shuttle Service" T-shirt he wore was too tight for his big body. As Ababio watched, Vern Junior stopped texting. He had something on his fingers. He put his phone down. He cleaned his fingers. They had some brown stuff on them. He left the tissue on the desk in front of him. Then he started texting again.

Betty Foster, an office worker, waved hello. "Hey Ababio," she said. Ababio smiled and waved back. She asked, "How's number 36 doing?"

Ababio shook his head. "Uh-oh," Betty said. "Not good."

Ababio went to Mr. Vernon Hackberry's desk. After a minute Mr. Hackberry looked up from his computer. He looked at Ababio. "Uh-huh," he said. He was a large man. His hair was cut short. His clothes were too tight for him.

"Mr. Hackberry," Ababio said, "shuttle bus number 36 may not start up again. That engine needs to be repaired."

Vernon Hackberry looked at Vern Junior's large back in the black T-shirt. "Vern Junior," Mr. Hackberry said.

"Yeah?" Vern Junior did not turn around. He kept texting.

"Go out and take a look at number 36, all right?" Mr. Hackberry said. Vern Junior did not answer. After a minute he got up. He put his phone away, and then went outside.

Ababio sighed. He went into the small break room to eat. He went to the refrigerator to get his lunch. Today it was a beautiful beef stew. He made it with friends from Ghana and Morocco the night before. They cooked beef and vegetables and spices in a beautiful brown sauce. He brought some to work for lunch today. He left it in the refrigerator with his name on it. But Ababio looked and looked and could not find it. His lunch was gone. "Oh no," he thought. "Not again."

Chapter 9

Kaleda Zia looked at the American lady who tapped her arm. "Hi," the woman said. "I think you bumped into me back there. Are you all right?"

"Yes," Kaleda said.

"What?" said the woman.

"Yes," Kaleda said.

The woman looked at Kaleda for a minute. Then she called out to the two workers, "Which of you needs a break?"

"It's my turn!" called the short African American woman. Her name tag said, "Daisy D., Moon Lake Coffee Barista."

"All right!" said the American lady. "Take the full ten minutes."

"Yes ma'am," said the young woman.

She took off her blue apron and left the coffee shop. The American lady put on a blue apron. Her name tag said, "Rebecca Mills, Moon Lake Coffee Manager." The lady Kaleda bumped into was a manager of Moon Lake Coffee.

Rebecca Mills looked at Kaleda. "Are you the new worker?"

"Yes," Kaleda said.

"Get on your apron. Start washing the dishes over there," Rebecca Mills said. She pointed at a sink full of dirty dishes.

"I don't have an apron," Kaleda said. "I forgot it."

"What?" Rebecca Mills said. The line of people waiting for coffee was very long. One man looked at his watch and left. A few women looked hard at the coffee shop workers. They were going to be late for their flights.

"I don't have an apron," Kaleda said.

Rebecca Mills was pouring a cup of coffee for a customer. She stopped what she was doing. She walked over to Kaleda and said, "I can't hear you. What did you say?"

Kaleda said, "I don't have an apron. I forgot it."

Rebecca Mills asked the other coffee shop worker, "Have you got an extra apron?"

The older female worker was quickly mixing coffee drinks. "Yeah," she said. "Just on the back of the door over there." She turned back to her work. She had long blonde hair pulled back from her face. Her name tag said, "Sharla M.,

Moon Lake Coffee Barista." She handed two coffee drinks to a customer. Another customer followed right behind in line.

Rebecca Mills went to the door and found the extra apron. "Put this on," she said to Kaleda. "Get started on those dishes, yes?" Kaleda put the blue Moon Lake Coffee apron on over her skirt and jacket. She started washing the dishes. She got all the dishes cleaned. She wiped them carefully with a towel. She put them away. More dirty dishes came. Kaleda washed and wiped them. Daisy came back from her break, and then Sharla took her break. When she came back, Daisy, Sharla, and Rebecca Mills worked together to fill orders. Little by little, the line of customers got shorter. People were getting their coffee and tea. They walked away to wherever they needed to go.

Kaleda had no more dishes to wash. She stood and waited for someone to tell her what to do. Rebecca Mills washed her hands. She turned to Kaleda. "Tell me your name," she said.

"Kaleda Zia," Kaleda said.

"Can I call you Kaleda?" Rebecca Mills said. Kaleda nodded her head a little.

"All right Kaleda. I'm glad you're working with us. You're new at this, right? You're new at this business? Well, welcome! But . . . if you're going to work in this shop, you're going to have to change the way you communicate," Rebecca Mills said. "Let's have some tea and talk about what you need to do to communicate better. We'll start with a lesson on tea." Rebecca Mills showed Kaleda how to make hot peppermint tea. "Our peppermint tea comes from Europe. It's organic," Rebecca Mills told her. "It's very pure. A lot of people come off their flights. They don't feel well. This tea really helps. I want you to try it. You need to learn about our drinks so you can sell them. And to sell, you have to communicate."

To Kaleda's surprise, the tea was very good.

Chapter 10

Wei Zhang was hungry. He had been working nonstop for five hours. He needed to get something to eat. His customer, an older man, said something to him. Wei Zhang said "Uh-huh." Then the customer said something again. He laughed and pointed at Wei Zhang's middle. Wei Zhang's stomach was rumbling. He was hungry, and his body wanted him to know it. When the massage was done, the older man thanked him. He gave Wei Zhang a five dollar cash tip. Then he reached into his pocket and pulled out a chocolate bar. He gave that to Wei Zhang, too. Wei Zhang laughed in surprise. But he was also very,

very happy. He really was hungry. He had not eaten since the day before.

It was now late October. Now there were only six men living in the dark apartment. Before, there had been twelve. Four of the men went back to China. They were homesick. They missed their families. They were tired of having so little money. They never went anywhere. None of them had a car. Another roommate simply left. No one knew where he went. But he took with him two of the men's cell phones. One other roommate left for a new job in Dallas. His ten months with AirSpa was done. Sometimes he texted Wei Zhang just to say hello. Yesterday he texted that his new boss was looking for another massage therapist. The money was good.

Was Wei Zhang interested? Wei Zhang answered that he wasn't sure. He still had four months left to work for AirSpa.

He could take this awful job for four more months, surely. He thought he could. But that thought didn't help him right now. The fact was, there was no food in the apartment. The bag of rice was gone. Wei Zhang had eaten a banana yesterday. It was a soft brown thing, almost bad. Wei Zhang ate it anyway. One of his roommates brought some green vegetables from a friend. They were also gone, eaten two days before.

Wei Zhang texted the AirSpa owner, who did not answer. The area around the apartment was just more and more apartments. Empty streets went in all directions. The way Wei Zhang remembered it, the closest food store was one and a half miles away. He had seen it from the bus at night, on the way home. He wondered if he could find it today. He had a little money now, with the five dollar cash tip. He had not been paid in three weeks. He wasn't sure how much he could buy. Maybe some of the other men could put their money together. They could buy more food that way.

Wei Zhang ate half of the chocolate bar. He took a little time to walk around the airport hall. He used the restroom. He washed his face. Then he decided he was finished for the day. He wasn't off for another two hours. But he had been working ten days straight, ten hours a day. He needed something more to eat.

He needed real food, some rice, some meat, some vegetables, some fruit. He needed to figure out how to get food for the apartment.

Thinking of these things, he saw the Chinese girl Min Li leave a nearby shop. She was dressed in a dark pink skirt and white top. Her beautiful black hair fell over her shoulders. Wei Zhang always wanted to talk to her. He saw her on the airport employee shuttle bus sometimes. But he was always too shy. She seemed high-class, educated. She had style. Wei Zhang's family back in Wuhan had a truck tire business. They had money. But no one ever thought to go to college. Min Li walked past Wei Zhang, down the airport hall.

He started back to AirSpa to get his

things to leave. He heard voices coming from ahead. Then he heard some shouts. What was happening? A crowd of people was standing in front of AirSpa. Wei Zhang saw some men and women in dark jackets go into the shop. The backs of their jackets said "US Department of . . ." Wei Zhang understood that part. He didn't know the one word below it. He read the letters L-A-B-O-R. Were they officers, like at the security checkpoint? The four AirSpa workers from the shop stood in the hall, watching the officers. They held their few things, their cell phones, a few dollars.

"What's happening?" Wei Zhang asked one of them.

"Trouble," the worker said. "I think we're out of a job."

Chapter 11

Wei Zhang could not understand what was happening. Travelers were standing around and watching. There were six officers in the AirSpa shop. They were putting things in boxes. Wei Zhang could see one female officer put credit card slips into a box. The box said: "US Department of Labor." Wei Zhang didn't know what the last word meant. What was "Labor"? Three more officers stood outside, in the airport hall. They were trying to talk to Wei Zhang and the other AirSpa workers. But like Wei Zhang, none of the workers knew very much English. None of the officers spoke Chinese.

Wei Zhang felt someone touch his

arm. He turned. Min Li stood there. She asked in Chinese, "What's happening? Are you OK?" She sounded like a girl from Wuhan, or any other small city. Wei Zhang was so surprised he couldn't answer. First, Min Li was so beautiful. Second, most of the time she acted like she didn't know Wei Zhang was alive. Wei Zhang didn't speak. Finally, Min Li said, "I'll talk to the officers for you."

Min Li talked to the officers for a long time. Then Min Li turned to the AirSpa workers and said in Chinese, "These officers are from the US Department of Labor. Their job is to protect workers."

One of Wei Zhang's co-workers said, "But we have passports. Our visas are still good!"

Min Li answered, "Yes, I know. These officers don't care about that. They're not immigration officers. Their job is to make sure workers are being paid. That their workplaces are safe."

"Then what do they want?" Wei Zhang asked.

"I think the owner of AirSpa is cheating you of tips," Min Li said. "There are two kinds of tips, right? One is cash tips where the customer just gives you cash money, like a ten dollar bill. The second kind comes from customers' credit card slips. Let's say AirSpa charges fifty dollars for a massage you give. The customer can still add ten dollars to that and then pay the sixty dollar charge with their credit card. Your boss should be giving you those tips at the end of each month."

Wei Zhang and his co-workers together said, "Ohhhhh . . ." They had never gotten any credit card tips.

"Well," Min Li said, "someone called the US Department of Labor and told them about it. So the officers came here today. They wanted to catch the owner, I think. Maybe they thought he would be here."

"I tried texting the owner four or five times," Wei Zhang said. "We haven't been paid, and we're out of food."

Min Li looked at Wei Zhang for a long time. Then she said, "The owner has escaped to China. I guess he's taken your money with him." One of the officers spoke quickly to Min Li. Then Min Li said, "The officer here needs your names and your phone numbers. You might still get some money."

Wei Zhang and his co-workers were completely quiet. They could not believe what was happening.

Min Li touched Wei Zhang's arm again. She gave him a small white card. "This is the name and address of the church I belong to. Some of us are Chinese, with some Vietnamese, Korean, and Taiwanese people, too. It's not far from the airport. We have food. We can help you out. Things like this happen all the time. Someone has bad luck. Or they work for a bad boss like yours. Just call that phone number. Someone will answer."

She walked away. Wei Zhang watched her. His mouth hung open. Then he looked at his co-workers. They looked at him. Wei Zhang gave them the name, address, and phone number of Min Li's church. He gave his name and phone number to the officers. He could do that, with his little bit of English. Then he left the airport. He went to the airport employee shuttle bus stop and waited for a shuttle bus. He got out his cell phone and texted his friend: "Yes, I am interested in that job. Where should I go? At what time?" He got an answer in less than a minute. His friend would pick him up at the old, dirty apartment. Wei Zhang would never stay there again.

Chapter 12

Rosa Maria and Elizabeth Carter had a shop full of customers. It seemed everyone wanted something to read. Rosa sold a storybook to a man with a small child. Then she sold a romance novel to a lady wearing a pink sweater. Elizabeth Carter, the owner of V.S. Carter Booksellers, sold fashion magazines to some American college girls. They were on their way to Mexico City to study cooking. When the girls had gone, Elizabeth Carter said, "I wonder what they plan to do with fashion magazines in Mexico City." She laughed.

"Well," Rosa said, "Perhaps that will get them interested in Mexican fashion magazines. They'll finish reading the ones they just bought. Then they'll be looking for something new. Any bookstore in Mexico City will have *Vanidades*, or *Glamour México*."

Elizabeth Carter put her head to one side. "Huh . . . interesting."

"That's how I got interested in learning English," Rosa said. "My uncle brought an American fashion magazine with him on a visit. I was fourteen. I loved the photos and the clothing and the makeup. I really started studying English then."

"Ah . . ." Elizabeth Carter said. "I wonder if we could have a copy or two to sell here. What were the names of the magazines again?" She picked up a pen and wrote the names Rosa gave her.

It had been a good month for Rosa.

She liked her job at the bookstore. Her English classes at the West River Community College were fine. Her nursing books were still hard to read. But her English teacher was helping her learn and use the words she needed. She had a new dictionary app that was helping, too. She was getting faster at using it. At her uncle's home, she had her own room. She could study there. And she had a new friend. Ababio Ollennu had found her West River Community College library book on the shuttle bus. He talked to Min Li. Did she know who had lost a library book? Then Min Li introduced Ababio to Rosa. Rosa got her library book back. Rosa liked Ababio. He was kind, funny, and smart. They texted every day. Last week, he came for lunch at Rosa's uncle's house. Uncle Roberto and Ababio talked for almost an hour about car and truck engine repair.

The front window of the V.S. Carter Booksellers bookstore looked different than it had the month before. Rosa cleaned the dark and dusty front window. The glass was clear now. You could see inside. Rosa took out all the books from the front window. She wiped up the dust. Then she used a fresh light green paint on the bookshelves. She painted the wall behind the bookshelves an even lighter shade of green. It looked interesting and bright. When you walked by, the fresh green caught your eye. Elizabeth Carter bought brighter lights to put in the front window. Once the paint was dry, Rosa and Elizabeth Carter discussed how to show books in the window. They decided to show travel books in both English and Spanish. Elizabeth Carter added the top five bestseller books for that week. At the last minute, she added two Texas cooking cookbooks. She said, "Someone visiting here might want to buy one to take back home."

"Uh-huh," Rosa said.

Elizabeth Carter went over to the two large reading chairs. A customer was sitting there reading a book. "Let me know if I can help you find anything," said Elizabeth Carter. The customer, an older woman, said, "Yes, thanks." Then she went back to reading. Rosa and her boss had pulled the two large chairs from the back room. They were soft and comfortable. Once Rosa wiped them off with a damp towel, you could see the chairs were a rich brown velvet. They were so soft. The two women put the chairs next to a table. Customers could sit down and read for as long as they liked.

As the two women closed V.S. Carter Booksellers for the day, Rosa got a text. It was Ababio. The text read "I need your help with a top-secret project!"

She texted back, "What project?"

In a minute, Ababio texted back with, "Do you know where I can buy chicken feet?"

Chapter 13

Rebecca Mills was speaking to Kaleda Zia in the back room of Moon Lake Coffee number seven. Rebecca Mills was angry. Her eyes were wide. Her cheeks were pink. But she kept her voice low. She said "Kaleda, you were doing so well. You were talking louder. You were communicating better. You were learning how to be a good barista. Your coffee and tea drinks were tasting better. But then this!"

Kaleda just looked at Ms. Mills. Her face was blank. She said nothing.

Rebecca Mills said, "Do you understand what you did?"

Kaleda still said nothing. She did not move. She just looked at Ms. Mills.

"OK," Ms. Mills said. "You're going back to your old ways. You're not saying or doing anything. Your face is as blank as an empty coffee cup. These are not going to help you in the working world. So let's try this. I will say something. Then all you have to do is nod your head for 'yes.' If you want to say 'no' you can shake your head. All right?"

Kaleda nodded her head "yes." She was wearing her usual dark clothes. Her hijab was dark blue. A piece of her hair had come out of her hijab. She didn't notice it.

"All right," Rebecca Mills said. "This morning we had a large order of milk coming to the store. I told you about this yesterday. Do you remember that?"

Kaleda nodded her head.

"We need the milk to make our coffee and tea drinks, yes? We need regular milk, cream, soy milk, and almond milk, yes? Our customers like those. But this morning, we have no milk. We can only make coffee or tea without milk. You know this, right?"

Kaleda nodded her head.

Rebecca Mills said, "The milk delivery man called me an hour ago. He said you wouldn't talk to him. Daisy and Sharla were on break, so it was just you in the store. Does that sound right?"

Kaleda finally spoke. "I didn't know what he wanted."

Ms. Mills said, "I'm glad to hear you talking again Kaleda." Then she waited.

After a long minute Kaleda said, "I just froze. I was alone. The man came in.

He started talking. I didn't know what he wanted."

"Well, what happened was the milk delivery man tried to leave the milk order. But then he gave up. You weren't trying to communicate with him. He thought maybe there was a mistake with the order. Maybe the milk order needed to go to another Moon Lake Coffee shop in the airport. Now, Moon Lake Coffee shop number two has *our* order. And *we* have no milk. Now I have to go over there and try to get our milk order."

Kaleda said, "I'm very sorry."

"I'll tell you what," Ms. Mills said. "I'm going over to get our milk order. That will take me about forty-fiive minutes. I want you to go outside. I want you to take time to think. Do you really want to work at Moon Lake Coffee? Is this job what you want?"

Kaleda said "OK," in a small voice. She took off her blue apron and got her bag. She kept her head down. She didn't bump into anyone. She walked out through the Dallas/Fort Worth International Airport employee security checkpoint. Now she was in bright sunshine. She walked across the airport road where she saw a spot with green grass. She sat down on the grass. She thought and thought and thought. She felt sad. Her face lost that blank look. Now her face looked sad. Her mouth turned down. Kaleda started to cry. All her hope was gone. She missed home. It would be so easy to call her mother and father. Tell them what happened about failing her

MA program. She wanted to be a success in the United States! She had worked so hard! It was too soon to give up. She wanted to return to her studies. Perhaps she could try another school? But to do that, she needed a job.

Finally, her thoughts slowed down. Kaleda just breathed. She waited. She heard airplanes and cars and shuttles. Then she heard a smaller, sweeter sound. It was the sound of a living thing. It was a small singing cricket in the grass. Even in this busy airport, a small insect was singing. And soon, Kaleda's heart made a small, quiet song, too.

Kaleda made up her mind. She wanted to keep the job at Moon Lake Coffee. She would tell Rebecca Mills that. She would find a way to stay.

Chapter 14

Ababio Ollennu and Rosa Maria Garza had the afternoon off. It was Monday. After her morning English class at West River Community College, Rosa met Ababio at the main building of the college. He was a few minutes late. He came out of the building and smiled at Rosa.

Rosa asked, "What were you doing?"

Ababio answered, "Oh, I had an appointment in the main office. Just an interview. I'll tell you about it later."

She said, "A mystery! Very good. So what's up? You want to buy some . . . what . . . *chicken feet?*"

"Oh yes," Ababio said. "I have a special project."

Rosa laughed. "What project?"

"It's another mystery!" Ababio laughed.

After getting Ababio's text, Rosa asked Uncle Roberto's pretty wife where she could buy some chicken feet. She said the local *carniceria* (Spanish for "meat shop") had them. Ababio and Rosa took Ababio's little car to buy the chicken feet. They bought twenty of them. Rosa and her family in Puebla had eaten chicken feet many times. They were very good, if you cooked them right. Rosa was surprised that people in Ghana ate them, too. She knew that many Americans hated the idea. It was true that chicken feet looked sort of bad. They were big and yellow. You had to clean them well before cooking them.

At home, Ababio cooked the chicken

feet in a large frying pan. He added a large handful of red spice mix. He said it was salt, black pepper, red pepper, and some other "special things."

"Okay," Rosa said. "But now you must tell me what you are going to do with these."

Ababio smiled his big white smile. "I'm going to eat them, of course! But here are eight to take home with you. The rest, I'm taking to work tomorrow for my friends in the airport shuttle service office."

"Oh! Will they eat chicken feet?!?" Rosa asked.

"Of course! *Someone* there *really* likes my lunches," Ababio said.

The next morning Ababio arrived at work with a big bag of his delicious chicken feet. He wrapped the bag in a cloth. He walked in and saw Betty, Mr. Vernon Hackberry, and Vern Junior. Mr. Hackberry was talking on the phone. Vern Junior didn't look up. He was texting.

Betty said, "Good morning! What's that?"

"Oh," Ababio said, "just another of my *delicious* lunches!" He went into the break room and put the chicken feet in the refrigerator.

Betty handed him the keys for a shuttle bus. She said, "You'll be working the airport employee parking lot."

Ababio looked at the shuttle bus keys. "Oh no, this is number 36!" he said. "Is that shuttle bus even alive? Will it even start?"

Betty said, "Mr. Hackberry says that Vern Junior got it running again."

Ababio looked at the keys and shook his head. "All right," he said. "We will see." He found shuttle bus number 36. It was still old and tired. It still smelled like old fried food. Ababio put the key in and turned it. Nothing happened. He tried again. Still nothing. He thought shuttle bus number 36 was truly dead now.

Ababio went back into the airport shuttle service office. He needed to tell Mr. Hackberry that number 36 would not start. As he opened the office door he heard shouting. Then he heard a crashing sound. It came from the break room. Someone had dropped something. Ababio smiled. He walked into the break room to find Vern Junior staring at a bag full of delicious yellow chicken feet on the floor. Betty and Mr. Hackberry stood looking at Vern Junior. Then they looked at the bag of chicken feet.

Ababio reached over and picked up the bag. Then he took out a chicken foot and slowly ate one. "Ummmm, good," he said. Vern Junior ran out of the room. "Got you, you big lunch thief," Ababio said to the empty door.

Chapter 15

Today was Ababio Ollennu's last day working at the Dallas/Fort Worth International Airport. It was late November. Tomorrow he would fly to Ghana for a visit. He was looking forward to seeing his family. He even wanted to see his cousin Folami. He wondered what Folami would think of his chicken feet trick on Vern Junior. After three weeks Ababio would return to Dallas for his new job. He was a new instructor of physics at West River Community College!

Vern Junior never came back to the airport shuttle service office. Mr. Vernon Hackberry apologized to both Ababio and Betty. Vern Junior had been stealing Ababio's and Betty's lunches all this time. Mr. Hackberry gave Ababio and Betty some 20 percent discount cards for a restaurant owned by his friend. "I'm sorry my son is so stupid," he said.

Ababio saw Betty roll her eyes, just a little. Later, Betty told Ababio that she had never laughed so hard. "The look on Vern Junior's face!" she said. And she had tried one of the chicken feet. "It's weird, but I kind of like it," she had said.

It turned out shuttle bus number 36 was not dead. Mr. Hackberry got a good mechanic to look at it. The shuttle was running again. The engine had a soft, smooth rumble. Mr. Hackberry had shuttle bus number 36 cleaned inside. The fried food smell was gone. Ababio was driving number 36 today. He was taking airport employees to the security checkpoint. Mr. Hasim said, "Oh, that engine is sounding better today."

"That's right, man!" Ababio said.

In a few minutes, a woman got on the shuttle bus. The woman said, "Hello."

Ababio looked at her in surprise. It was the quiet lady from Bangladesh.

"Hello," Ababio said. "How are you doing?"

"Very well, thank you," said the lady.

She was talking louder. Her face was no longer blank. She looked Ababio in the eye. She wore her usual hijab and glasses. But her clothes were lighter in color. Today she wore a gray skirt and a very light purple shirt. Around her neck she wore an airport employee name tag. It said, "Kaleda Z., Moon Lake Coffee

Barista." Kaleda Zia walked to the back of the shuttle bus and sat down.

Then Ababio saw the person he was waiting for. Rosa Maria Garza got on shuttle bus number 36. With her was Min Li. Both women were on their way to work. Both had just come from their English class at West River Community College. They were still talking about college.

"Can you believe it?" Min Li was saying. "Wei Zhang has started taking English classes, too. He's taking 'community English' at school."

Rosa laughed. "Why are you so surprised?" she asked.

Min Li said, "He's so stubborn. I never thought he would learn English."

Ababio broke in and said, "Wei is stubborn? How do you know that?"

Min Li turned a little pink and said, "Oh, I just know."

Both Ababio and Rosa laughed. Rosa and Min Li sat on the seat at the front of the bus so they could talk to Ababio. They had to wait for more airport employees before Ababio drove the shuttle to the airport employee security checkpoint.

Min Li told Ababio more about Wei Zhang. Wei Zhang's boss, the owner of AirSpa, was still in China. But the US Department of Labor found that the owner had been stealing his massage therapists' credit card tips. The officers closed the owner's bank accounts in the US. Wei Zhang had gotten eight thousand dollars! These were the credit card tips Wei Zhang had worked so many months for.

Min Li said that Wei Zhang liked his new job. It was owned by a Chinese American woman. It was hard work. But she paid fairly. The new massage spa was close to a large, beautiful, old department store in downtown Dallas. Min Li had interviewed for a job there last week. She had stopped by to visit Wei Zhang.

"Ah," Ababio said. "You may be working in a new place before long."

"Maybe!" said Min Li. "A new place . . . that would be good. I would like that. I used to be scared of doing new things. I was scared of being new." Then she looked at each of her friends. "Because of you, I am not scared anymore."

Printed in the USA
CPSIA information can be obtained
at www.ICGtesting.com
LVHW042311280823
756565LV00026B/251

9 781956 476248